MURMEL, MURMEL, MURMEL

MURMEL, MURMEL, MURMEL

Story
Robert Munsch

Art
Michael Martchenko

Annick Press Ltd.
Toronto • New York

Eighteenth printing, October 1996

Annick Press Ltd.

Annick Press gratefully acknowledges the support of the
Canada Council and the Ontario Arts Council.

Canadian Cataloguing in Publication Data
  Munsch, Robert N., 1945-
    Murmel, murmel, murmel

(Munsch for kids)
ISBN 0-920236-29-4 (bound) ISBN 0-920236-31-6 (pbk.)

I. Martchenko, Michael. II. Title. III. Series:
Munsch, Robert N., 1945-   . Munsch for kids.

Ps8576.U58M87   jC813'.54   C82-094731-8
PZ7.M86Mu

Distributed in Canada by:
Firefly Books Ltd.
3680 Victoria Park Avenue
Willowdale, ON
M2H 3K1

Published in the U.S.A. by Annick Press (U.S.) Ltd.
Distributed in the U.S.A. by:
Firefly Books (U.S.) Inc.
P.O. Box 1338
Ellicott Station
Buffalo, NY 14205

 Printed on acid-free paper.

Printed and bound in Canada by Friesens.

To Andrew, Julie, Robin and Andrea

When Robin went out into her back yard, there was a large hole right in the middle of her sandbox. She knelt down beside it and yelled, "ANYBODY DOWN THERE?"

From way down the hole something said, "Murmel, murmel, murmel."

"Hmmm," said Robin, "very strange." So she yelled, even louder, "ANYBODY DOWN THERE?"

"Murmel, murmel, murmel," said the hole. Robin reached down the hole as far as she could and gave an enormous yank. Out popped a baby.

"Murmel, murmel, murmel," said the baby.

"Murmel, yourself," said Robin. "I am only five years old and I can't take care of a baby. I will find somebody else to take care of you."

Robin picked up the very heavy baby and walked down the street. She met a woman pushing a baby carriage. Robin said, "Excuse me, do you need a baby?"

"Heavens, no," said the woman. "I already have a baby." She went off down the street and seventeen diaper salesmen jumped out from behind a hedge and ran after her.

Robin picked up the baby and went on down the street. She met an old woman and said, "Excuse me, do you need a baby?"

"Does it pee its pants?" said the old lady.

"Yes," said Robin.

"Yecch," said the old lady. "Does it dirty its diaper?"

"Yes," said Robin.

"Yecch," said the old lady. "Does it have a runny nose?"

"Yes," said Robin.

"Yecch," said the old lady. "I already have seventeen cats. I don't need a baby." She went off down the street. Seventeen cats jumped out of a garbage can and ran after her.

Robin picked up the baby and went down the street. She met a woman in fancy clothes. "Excuse me," said Robin, "do you need a baby?"

"Heavens, no," said the woman. "I have seventeen jobs, lots of money and no time. I don't need a baby." She went off down the street. Seventeen secretaries, nine messengers and a pizza delivery man ran after her.

"Rats," said Robin. She picked up the baby and walked down the street. She met a man. "Excuse me," she said, "do you need a baby?"

"I don't know," said the man. "Can it wash my car?"

"No," said Robin.

"Can I sell it for lots of money?"

"No," said Robin.

"Well, what is it for?" said the man.

"It is for loving and hugging and feeding and burping," said Robin.

"I certainly don't need that," said the man. He went off down the street. Nobody followed him.

Robin sat down beside the street, for the baby was getting very heavy.

"Murmel, murmel, murmel," said the baby.

"Murmel, yourself," said Robin. "What am I going to do with you?"

An enormous truck came by and stopped.

A truck driver jumped out and walked around Robin three times. Then he looked at the baby.

"Excuse me," said Robin, "do you need a baby?"

The truck driver said, "Weeeellll..."

"Murmel, murmel, murmel," said the baby.

"Did you say, 'murmel, murmel, murmel'?" asked the truck driver.

"Yes!" said the baby.

"I need you," yelled the truck driver. He picked up the baby and started walking down the street.

"Wait," said Robin, "you forgot your truck!"

"I already have seventeen trucks," said the truck driver. "What I need is a baby..."

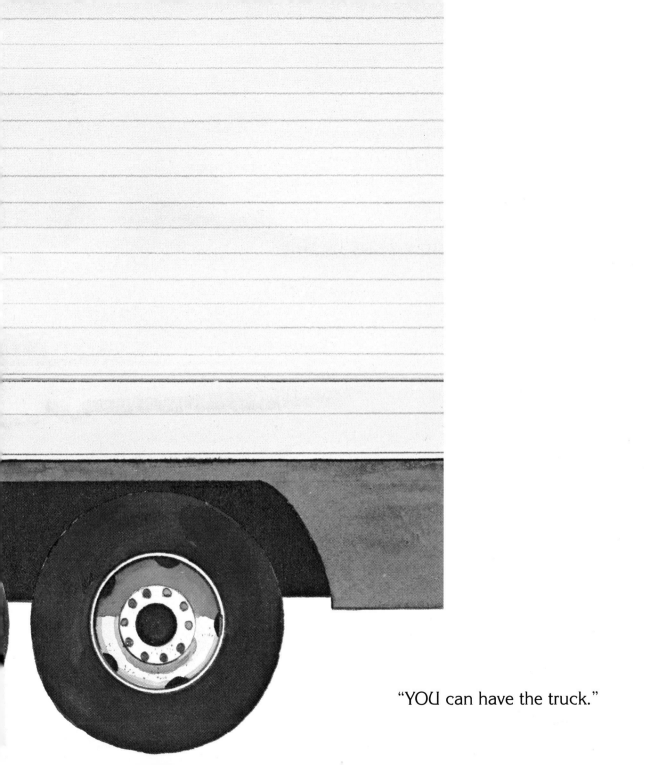

"YOU can have the truck."

Other books in the Munsch for Kids series:

The Dark
Mud Puddle
The Paper Bag Princess
The Boy in the Drawer
Jonathan Cleaned Up, Then He Heard a Sound
Millicent and the Wind
Mortimer
The Fire Station
Angela's Airplane
David's Father
Thomas' Snowsuit
50 Below Zero
I Have to Go!
Moira's Birthday
A Promise is a Promise
Pigs
Something Good
Show and Tell
Purple, Green and Yellow
Wait and See
Where is Gah-Ning?
From Far Away
Stephanie's Ponytail

Many Munsch titles are available in French and/or
Spanish. Please contact your favourite supplier.